JACK RUSSELL: Dog Detective

The Sausage Situation

DARREL & SALLY ODGERS

SCHOLASTIC CANADA LTD.

New York Toronto London Auckland Sydney
Mexico City New Delhi Hong Kong Buenos Aires

Scholastic Canada Ltd.

604 King Street West, Toronto, Ontario M5V 1E1, Canada

Scholastic Inc.

557 Broadway, New York, NY 10012, USA

Scholastic Australia Pty Limited

PO Box 579, Gosford, NSW 2250, Australia

Scholastic New Zealand Limited

Private Bag 94407, Greenmount, Auckland, New Zealand

Scholastic Children's Books

Euston House, 24 Eversholt Street, London NW1 1DB, UK

Library and Archives Canada Cataloguing in Publication

Odgers, Darrel

The sausage situation / Darrel & Sally Odgers;
illustrations by Janine Dawson.
(Jack Russell, dog detective ; #6)
ISBN 978-0-545-99932-8

I. Odgers, Sally, 1957-   II. Dawson, Janine   III. Title.
IV. Series. Odgers, Darrel. Jack Russell, dog detective ; #6.
PZ7.O2374Sau 2007   j823'.92   C2007-901001-6

First published by Scholastic Press in 2006.
Text copyright © 2006 by Sally and Darrel Odgers.
Cover design copyright © 2006 Lake Shore Graphics.
Dog, Frisbee, courtesy of the Cansick family.
Interior illustrations by Janine Dawson.
Interior illustrations copyright © 2006 Scholastic Australia.
ISBN-10 0-545-99932-4

6 5 4 3 2 1   Printed in Canada   07 08 09 10 11

Dear Readers,

The story you're going
to read is about me and my
friends, and how we sorted
out the Sausage Situation. To save
time, I'll introduce us all to you now.
Of course, if you know us already, you
can trot off to Chapter One.

I am Jack Russell, Dog Detective.
I live with my landlord, Sarge, in
Doggeroo. Sarge detects human-type
crimes. I have the important job of
detecting crimes that deal with dogs.
I'm a Jack Russell terrier, so I am
dogged and intelligent.

Next door to Sarge and me live
Auntie Tidge and Foxy. Auntie Tidge is
lovely. She has dog biscuits. Foxy is not
lovely. He's a fox terrier (more or less).

1

He used to be a street dog and a thief, but he's reformed now. Auntie Tidge has even gotten rid of his fleas. Foxy sometimes helps me with my cases.

Uptown Lord Setter (Lord Red for short) lives in Uptown House with Caterina Smith. Lord Red means well, but he isn't very bright.

We have other friends in Doggeroo. These include Polly the dachshund, Jill Russell, the squekes, Ralf Boxer, and Shuffle the pug. Then there's Fat Molly Cat from the library.

That's all you need to know, so let's begin the first chapter.

Yours doggedly,

Jack Russell—the detective with a nose for crime.

Smelling Sausages

The Sausage Situation began on a day
when crime was a long way from my
mind.

I was thinking of something very
important. Jill Russell's people had
invited me to spend a few days at
their place.

When Sarge came out to the
porch, I did the **paw thing**. I was
telling Sarge it was time to go to Jill
Russell's.

"You're not coming with me today,
Jack," said Sarge. "I'm going to the
school to give a talk on highway safety."

I rolled my eyes.

Jack's Facts

*All dogs know exactly how to make
their people feel guilty.
Nice dogs do this only when their
people deserve it.
I am a nice dog.
This is a fact.*

"Sorry, Jack." Sarge patted my head.

I sighed. Then I wagged my tail
five times, to show I forgave him.

After Sarge had gone, I lay down
to wait. After quite a while, I saw two
paws poking through a hole under
the hedge.

"Who goes there?" I demanded.

The paws **pawsed**.

"I know it's you, Foxy," I said.

"Why are you sneaking around?"

Foxy **ig-gnawed** that. He came up onto my porch. "Auntie Tidge is cleaning the freezer in the kitchen. She sent me out. Let's go and visit Jill Russell."

"We can't go today, and you're not invited, anyway," I said.

Foxy sulked. "Auntie Tidge planted some lettuce. Let's dig it up."

"That's no fun," I said. "You can't play with lettuce. You'll get dirt in your teeth."

"You can always—" Foxy stopped suddenly and sniffed the air.

"What is it?" I asked.

Foxy sniffed harder and started to drool. He had smelled something. I quickly made a **nose map**.

5

Jack's Map

1. My empty dinner bowl.

2. Foxy.

3. A van.

4. Auntie Tidge.

5. Strange man.

6. Sausages.

"Sausages!" said Foxy. He jumped up and scooted back to his own yard.

Jack's Facts

All dogs depend on their noses.
Jack Russells use their other senses as
well. This is why Jack Russells are
su-paw-rior.
This is a fact.

The sausage scent was coming from the road outside Auntie Tidge's house.

I heard a door slam. *That must be the van I had nose-mapped,* I thought.

I heard the latch on Foxy's gate click open.

I heard a strange man speaking. "Here are your sausages, **Miss Russell.**

1

Where do you want them?"

"In the kitchen, Mr. Beale," said Auntie Tidge. "I'll put them in the freezer. Foxy Woxy, no! Down!"

I heard the strange man yell. I **Jack-jumped** to look over the fence and saw he had tripped over Foxy.

Foxy was still sniffing loudly.

The sausage scent was getting stronger.

"No, Foxy, no! *Bad dog*! No!" Auntie Tidge sounded upset.

We had a **situation** here. It was some kind of Sausage Situation. Auntie Tidge was in trouble!

Jack Russell's the name, detection's the game! I went to rescue her.

Auntie Tidge was sitting on the garden path in the yard with her legs stuck out in front of her. I **greeted** her to make sure she was all right. The strange man was yelling at Foxy.

There were boxes scattered on the ground. One had burst open. Foxy had his head right inside it, and I could hear him guzzling and gulping.

I didn't need a nose map to tell me Foxy was feasting on sausages.

Jack's Facts

Human-type food does not belong on the ground.
Therefore, eating human-type food that has fallen on the ground is not stealing.
It is cleaning up a mess.
This is a fact.

I was about to help Foxy clean up the mess when Sarge came up the path. He shut Foxy in the shed and sent me home.

Jack's Glossary

Paw thing. *Up on hind legs, paws held together as if praying. Means pleased excitement.*

Pawsed. *Stopped to think, done by a dog.*

Ig-gnawed. *Ignored, but done by dogs.*

Nose map. *Way of storing information collected by the nose.*

Su-paw-rior. *Superior, the way Jack Russells are.*

Jack's Glossary

Miss Russell. *I am Jack Russell. Sarge is Sergeant Russell. Auntie Tidge is Miss Russell.*

Jack-jump. *A sudden jump made by a Jack Russell terrier.*

Situation. *Something of interest to a dog detective.*

Greet. *This is done by rising to the hind legs and clutching a person with the paws while slurping their face.*

"Stop, Thief"

Foxy was still grumbling about the
Sausage Situation two days later.

"Those sausages are mine by
right," he kept saying. "They were on
the ground in my **terrier-tory**!"

"I know. You were guzzling them,"
I said.

"I only had three. Auntie Tidge hid
the rest before she let me out of the
shed."

"That's so you wouldn't eat them
all at once and get sick." I was tired of

hearing about the Sausage Situation.
I had other things on my mind.

"Foxy Woxy! **Jackie Wackie!**"
called Auntie Tidge from Foxy's house.

"She's going to give us sausages!"
yelped Foxy. He shot home. I
followed. Maybe Auntie Tidge was
going to take me to Jill Russell's place.
She takes me out sometimes when
Sarge is busy at work.

Auntie Tidge had the boxes
of sausages stacked on the table.
Even my **super-sniffer** had trouble
detecting them, because they were so
cold. They must have been stored in
the freezer.

Auntie Tidge caught Foxy as he
dashed past, and she picked up a brush.

"Keep still, Foxy Woxy. I want to make you look handsome." She leashed him to a chair leg, and brushed him smooth. Then she brushed me. She patted us and got up. "Wait here, boys. I have to pop over to Dora's before we go."

"Before we go *where*?" I asked Foxy when Auntie Tidge had gone out. "Are we going to Jill Russell's?"

Foxy ig-gnawed me. He was trying to climb up the leg of the table.

"Stop that," I said. "You'll have all the sausages on top of us."

"Good!" howled Foxy. "I will eat them *all*."

Above the noise Foxy was making, I heard a van stop outside.

I made a quick nose map.

Jack's Map

1. Foxy.

2. Sausages.

3. Auntie Tidge.

4. Lord Red.

5. Caterina Smith.

There was a knock on the door.
"Hello? Are you there, Auntie Tidge?"
It was Caterina Smith. She opened the
door and came in.

Foxy ig-gnawed her, so I growled a
warning.

Jack's Facts

It is a dog's duty to protect his terrier-tory.
If a dog neglects his duty, his pal must do
it for him.
Foxy was neglecting his duty.
This is a fact.

"Don't be silly, Jack," said Caterina
Smith. She picked up the boxes of
sausages and carried them out the door.

"She's stealing my sausages!" yelped
Foxy. "Stop her, Jack!"

Foxy was tied to the chair leg, so I leaped into action and darted through the **dog door** in pursuit. I couldn't stop Caterina Smith, but I *could* follow her and **monitor the situation**.

Behind me, I heard a **terrier-able** noise. It was Foxy, dragging the chair behind him. He tried to get out the dog door behind me. There was an even more terrier-able noise as the chair hit the door.

"Stop, thief!" bawled Foxy as I ran down the path and through the gate.

Caterina Smith's van was parked by the curb. She opened the side door and slid the pile of boxes inside. I saw Lord Red peering out the rear window. Was Lord Red an accessory to this crime? I could hardly believe it!

"Stop, in the name of the paw!" I ordered. I grabbed Caterina Smith by the hem of her skirt and tugged. "Those are Auntie Tidge's sausages."

Caterina Smith looked down at me and frowned. "Back you go, Jack. I'm in a hurry." She pulled me off her skirt, pushed me back through the gate, and closed it behind me.

Of course, I didn't stay in the yard. I got out (never mind how) just as Caterina Smith drove away with the sausages.

Jack's Glossary

Terrier-tory. *A territory owned by a terrier.*

Jackie Wackie. *Auntie Tidge is the only person allowed to call me that.*

Super-sniffer. *Jack's nose in super-sniff mode.*

Dog door. *A door especially for dogs.*

Monitor the situation. *Keep close watch on something interesting.*

Terrier-able. *Same as terrible, but to do with terriers.*

FOLLOW That Van

"Follow that van, detective!" I told myself. "Don't let the thief get away!"

I dashed in pursuit, but not even a tracking Jack can keep up with a van being driven by a sausage thief. Jacks are fast and fearless, but I began to fall behind.

I was about to give up and turn back when the van stopped. Caterina Smith got out and picked me up.

"Bad dog, Jack! I wondered why Lordie was making such a fuss in the back. I can't leave you wandering around, so you'll just have to come with me."

I hoped she might put me with the boxes of stolen sausages so I could go on monitoring the situation. Instead, she bundled me into the backseat with Lord Red.

Red was **pawfully** pleased to see me. He bounced with excitement. His ears bounced, too. "Jack, Jack, are you coming to the Dog and Sausage Day with me, Jack? Are you? Why isn't Foxy coming, Jack? Doesn't he want to—"

"Stop it, Red!" I snapped. "One thing at a time. Don't you realize I'm being **dognapped**?"

Red stopped bouncing. "Dognapped? Who's dognapping you?"

"Caterina Smith," I explained.

"Caterina Smith isn't a dognapper, Jack. Besides, why would she dognap you? She's already got a dog. She's got me."

"First she stole some sausages, and now she's dognapped me because I was tracking her."

"You're not being dognapped, Jack, and Caterina Smith hasn't stolen anything."

"I am, and she has," I said. "I'm on the trail of the stolen sausages. Caterina Smith has—"

"Don't be silly, Jack," said Red. "Caterina Smith is bringing the sausages to Dog and Sausage Day. That's where we're going right now."

"But—" I stopped. Suddenly, I realized I might have gotten it wrong.

Jack's Facts

*Any dog that thinks he is always right
is often wrong.
A smart dog will admit that sooner
rather than later.
Jack Russells are smart dogs.
This is a fact.*

I considered the facts. Caterina
Smith is Auntie Tidge's friend. Maybe
Auntie Tidge had said she could have
the sausages. Maybe we really were
on our way to Dog and Sausage Day.
I wasn't sure. All I could do was
continue to monitor the situation.

"What's Dog and Sausage Day?"
I asked.

"It happens at the friendly school," said Red. "It's even more fun than a dog show! There are chew toys and ball games and a costume parade. Caterina Smith made me a costume. She says the kids will love me."

For the first time, I noticed Lord Red was wearing a red, stretchy sweater. It reached all the way from his shoulders back to his hind legs.

"What are you supposed to be?"
I asked. "A stocking?"

"I am dressed as a hot dog," said
Red.

I was about to **in-terrier-gate** Red
more when the van stopped at the school.

People and dogs were everywhere.
I saw Polly Smote with a ruffle around
her neck. Shuffle the pug had on a
little hat.

Caterina Smith left us in the van
while she carried the sausage boxes
away.

I was worried.

Jacks jump over.

Jacks burrow under.

Jacks squeeze through.

But not even a Jack can escape
from the backseat of a van.

How could I monitor the Sausage Situation from here?

Jack's Glossary

Pawfully. *Very; awfully.*

Dognapped. *Like kidnapped, but done to a dog.*

In-terrier-gate. *Official questioning, done by a terrier.*

Doggeroo Dog and Sausage Day

While I was still worrying, Auntie
Tidge's little car pulled up behind us.
The windows were closed, but I could
hear Foxy nagging Auntie Tidge about
the sausages. When he saw me in the
van, he almost jumped through the
windshield.

"I'll get you for this, Jack Russell!"

"What's wrong with Foxy?" asked Red.

"He thinks we've got those
sausages," I said.

Auntie Tidge let Foxy out. Foxy
dashed to the van and jumped up
and down.

"Sausages! Sausages! Sausages!" he yapped.

That was a mistake. All the other dogs had been trotting around with their people. When they heard what Foxy was yapping, they joined in.

The three squekes had been yipping around with their person, Dora Barkins. Then they heard Foxy.

"Sausages? Sausages! Where? Where? Where?" they yipped.

Polly **dached** up next. "Sausages? Did someone say sausages?" she demanded.

"Sausages!" Shuffle joined in.

Even Ralf Boxer, who is hardly as big as a sausage himself, started yapping.

Lord Red joined in. "Sausages! Sausages!"

Since I was shut in the van with him, his voice sounded terrier-ably loud.

"Stop that, Red!" I yelped.

Red stopped. The other dogs didn't. Their people started shouting.

Auntie Tidge grabbed Foxy.

"Sausages!" barked Foxy, leaping at the van again.

"They're not here!" I barked back. "We have a new situation! Caterina Smith took them away!"

"Where? Where?" Foxy pulled away from Auntie Tidge. "Someone's stealing my sausages again!" He darted off. Auntie Tidge let him go. She is not in the right shape for running.

She let me and Lord Red out of the van. "*There* you are, Jackie Wackie! I wish you wouldn't disappear like that. And now Foxy's done it, too. I don't know what's gotten into him today."

I knew. Three sausages and a big idea had got into Foxy. That was the trouble!

Caterina Smith came back without the sausages.

"All the dogs are being silly," said Auntie Tidge. "Jack and Lordie are the only ones who remember their manners."

I greeted Auntie Tidge for that. Then I got down to business. I had to find Foxy before he did something terrier-able.

I made a nose map.

Jack's Map

1. Lots of dogs.

2. Lots of people.

3. Auntie Tidge.

4. Lord Red.

5. *Caterina Smith.*

6. *Foxy.*

7. *Sausages.*

8. *Onions.*

The sausage scent was faint. So was the Foxy scent. The onion scent was strong. It seemed to be coming from a green tent. I set off across the school yard to investigate. Dogs had been playing ball games with kids. Now they were all racing around hunting for sausages instead.

I'd almost reached the green tent when Sarge called.

"Jack? Jack, come back here!"

Mostly, when Sarge calls, I answer.
It might be time for dinner, or a ball
game. It might be time to visit Jill
Russell.

This time, I ig-gnawed Sarge.
I raced around the side of the green
tent. People and dogs scattered as
I ran. I was a Jack on a mission.

I *had* to catch up with Foxy.

I stopped so suddenly that my paws skidded on the grass.

Why did I have to catch up with Foxy?

I sat down and shook my ears. Why should I monitor the Sausage Situation? They weren't *my* sausages. Auntie Tidge must have said Caterina Smith could take them. If Foxy was going to be terrier-able, why should I get involved?

I trotted back to Sarge.

Jack's Glossary

Dached. *The way dachshunds get around.*

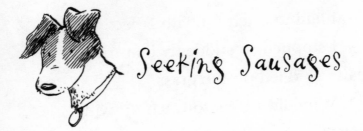

Seeking Sausages

"Hello, Jack," said Sarge. He patted me.
"Auntie says Foxy has upset all the
dogs and run off."

I **Jack-attacked** Sarge's leg to get
attention and **pointed** toward the
green tent.

"Over there, eh?" said Sarge.
"Trust Foxy to follow the food." He
looked at barking dogs and scolding
people and lifted his voice. "Control
your dogs!"

Everyone did as Sarge said.

<u>Jack's Facts</u>

Sarge is a police sergeant.
Police sergeants are like Jack Russell terriers.
When they give orders, people and dogs obey.
This is a fact.

Inside the tent there was a table stacked with sausage boxes. Jack and Jill Johnson from the station were cooking onions and buttering bread.

I sneezed. Then I remembered something. Where was Jill Russell? I couldn't believe I'd forgotten her. Jack and Jill Johnson were Jill Russell's people. So why wasn't she here?

I went to Jack Johnson. I did the

paw thing. Then I did the paw thing to Jill Johnson. I whined.

Jill Johnson laughed. "Jill Russell couldn't come today, Jack. She's safer at home." She waved her cooking tongs at Polly, who had followed us in. "Off you go, Polly. Onions are bad for dogs."

Polly snorted. "I don't want onions," she told me. "Why would I want onions? I want those sausages."

I looked up at the boxes. I looked down at Polly. Her legs were too short for her to jump up there.

"Go *away!*" Jill Johnson waved her tongs again.

The three squekes yipped through the door. "Sausages, sausages, sausages!" They all wore little stripy jackets. They looked like hairy wasps.

"Boys? Boys!" Dora Barkins ran in and scooped them up. "So sorry," she said.

"Don't worry, Dora. Half the dogs in Doggeroo have been looking for sausages in here. Somehow, they know what's in those boxes." Jill Johnson wagged her tongs at a bulldog wearing a baby bonnet. It had burrowed under the back flap of the tent.

"Have you seen Foxy?" asked Sarge. "Auntie is worried about him. My Jack seemed to think he was here."

"No," said Jill Johnson. "Your Jack just wants to see Jill Russell, or maybe eat sausages. Which is it, Jackie Wackie?"

I like Jill Johnson, but Auntie Tidge is the only person allowed to call me that.

I left the tent. Caterina Smith wasn't a thief or a dognapper, but now I had a mystery to solve.

Where was Foxy? I sat down and tried to make a nose map.

All I could smell was onions. With my super-sniffer out of action, I used my other senses. I got up on my hind legs and looked around. I Jack-jumped. I saw plenty of dogs. I saw three fox terriers. None was Foxy.

I pricked my ears. Most dogs had stopped barking. People talked and laughed. Birds twittered. Squekes yipped. I heard Sarge say good-bye to Jack and Jill Johnson. I couldn't hear Foxy.

"Jack, Jack!" Red charged across the grass. "What's going on, Jack?"

"I'm looking for Foxy."

"I'll help," said Red. "Where should we look, Jack?"

I didn't know. I'd expected Foxy to be in the tent. Maybe the onions had confused his **sniffer**? That wouldn't stop Foxy. Before I could say so, I heard a familiar voice.

"Lordie? Lordieeeee!"

"Got to go," said Red. "Caterina Smith is calling. Perhaps she has saved me a sausage."

After Red left, I checked the other tents in search of Foxy. There were no more sausages, but I found some deluxe doghouses and a pile of baskets. Then I detected bins of dog toys.

I was just wondering if Sarge and I might get a new **squeaker-bone** when Foxy sneaked behind the green tent.

"Halt!" I yipped. "Auntie Tidge
wants you."

"I'm doing something **im-paw-tant**."

"Howling about sausages is not
im-paw-tant," I said. Then I realized
Foxy wasn't howling anymore. He was
sneaking.

"There are sausage thieves about. I
am **steaking out** this tent to guard the
sausages Caterina Smith stole from
Auntie Tidge," Foxy said.

"Caterina Smith didn't steal sausages," I said. "No one stole sausages. There has been no crime, after all."

"She did so steal sausages," said Foxy. "Jack and Jill Johnson have them now. My sausages must be protected. There is going to be another theft!"

Jack's Glossary

Jack-attack. *Growling and biting and pulling at trouser legs. Very loud. Quite harmless.*

Pointed. *Smart dogs use their noses to point to things.*

Sniffer. *A dog's nose in tracking mode. Only Jack Russell terriers have super-sniffers.*

Squeaker-bone. *Item for exercising teeth. Not to be confused with a toy.*

Im-paw-tant. *Important, for dogs.*

Steak-out. *Hiding and watching for* **pupetrators** *(see next chapter).*

# Skulldoggery

"There haven't been any thefts," I said. "We made a mistake."

"I saw a bulldog sneak under the wall," said Foxy. "What does that say to you?"

"A sneaking bulldog is certainly up to **skulldoggery**," I agreed.

"Exactly," said Foxy. "That's why I set up this steak-out. Those sausages are going to disappear very soon."

"A bulldog won't get away with it," I objected. "They aren't smart enough."

"The bulldog isn't the only dog involved. There's a smaller dog as well," explained Foxy. "He is *very* smart. It's a cunning plan, Jack. One dog distracts Jack and Jill Johnson while the other prepares to remove the sausages."

I was amazed. While I had looked for Foxy, Foxy had steaked-out a crime-scene-to-be.

"When is this theft going down?" I asked. "Who else is a witness? How many **pupetrators** are involved?"

"Don't in-terrier-gate *me*," snapped Foxy. "In-terrier-gate the bulldog in the bonnet! These sausages must be saved!"

"Can you give a description of the other dog?"

"It's a smart, handsome, small dog," said Foxy.

"Stay here, then," I ordered. "I'll set up a steak-out near the door. These **canine criminals** can't get past two of us."

I knew the smaller pupetrator would be more difficult to catch, so I hid just outside the entrance of the tent. I listed suspects in my head. Foxy had said it was a small dog. This left out setters, spaniels, dalmatians, and Labradors.

Right, Jack, I asked myself. *What small dog* would *steal sausages?*

That was easy. Any dog that was not respectable.

That left a pawful lot of suspects.

Right, Jack, I thought. *What small dog* could *steal sausages?*

Before I could answer that, Polly Smote trotted past. It certainly wasn't her.

"Out you go, Polly," said Jill Johnson from inside the tent.

Polly trotted out again. "What do you want, Jack Russell?"

"I'm working on a case," I said. "Someone is going to steal sausages. When I catch the pupetrator I shall bark for backup."

"I'm not your pupetrator. Maybe it's him." Polly pointed her long dachshund nose at a dalmatian. It was creeping on its belly.

"That's not the thief," I said. "Jill Johnson will spot that dog easily."

"Out, darn Spot!" said Jill Johnson loudly.

"Told you," I said. "Besides, dalmatians are not small dogs."

"Who says the pupetrator is a small dog?" Polly wanted to know.

"Foxy. He has a steak-out around the back," I said.

"How could a small dog reach them?" Polly pointed at the sausage boxes.

"A clever small dog could do it," I

said. I crawled forward to look up at
the boxes. "I could Jack-jump that
high. I suspect the pupetrator may be
a terrier. Terriers are quick and clever."

I demonstrated my best Jack-jump
for Polly.

"I can see you, Jack Russell!" said
Jill Johnson. She wagged her tongs at
me. "Shoo, both of you!"

I backed away.

"Go!" said Jill Johnson.

Three spaniels wearing socks
slunk out of the tent.

Polly and I moved to a steak-out
behind the canvas flap, where Jill
Johnson could not see us.

"You're barking up the wrong tree
here," said Polly. "No dog is stealing
sausages."

Just then, the bulldog in the bonnet burrowed out from under the side of the tent. "Halt in the name of the paw!" I snapped. "Polly! Crime in progress! Back me up!"

I leaped forward to make an arrest.

Jack's Glossary

Skulldoggery. *Bad things concerning dogs.*

Pupetrator. *A criminal that happens to be a pup or a dog, or who does bad things to dogs.*

Canine criminals. *Bad dogs.*

Spreading the Word

The bulldog snarled. "I see a terrier toothpick." (A common insult to terriers.)

"I see a bulldog in a bonnet." (A not-so-common reply to a bulldog.)

"What do you want, toothpick?"

"I'm arresting you on suspicion of sausage theft," I said.

"Not guilty," said the bulldog.

"We have a situation, bulldog. Sausages are being stolen from here."

"Not guilty," repeated the bulldog.

"You can't deny you were crawling under the tent with intent to steal."

"Of paws I don't deny it. Any bulldog will crawl after sausages."

"And you haven't succeeded?" I demanded.

"Not a sausage," said the bulldog.

Polly sniffed with her long dachshund nose. "He's telling the truth, Jack. He's been eating hot dogs and pie, not sausages."

I was about to let the bulldog go when I remembered something. "You admit to attempted theft," I said. "Who is your partner in crime?"

"Bulldogs don't have partners. We have **henchdogs**."

"Who is your henchdog, then?"

The bulldog showed his fangs. Some dogs would have laughed at his bonnet. I am not like that. I told the bulldog he was **pawfectly** free to go.

"That's silly, Jack Russell," said Polly. "What bulldog would work with a small dog? Bulldogs use small dogs as toothpicks."

She had a point.

Jack's Facts

A smart detective can admit to a mistake, especially if it is someone else's mistake.
Jack Russells are the smartest detectives around.
This is a fact.

"I think Foxy is lying," said Polly.

I went to Foxy's steak-out. Foxy was not there.

Why would Foxy lie? Did he want to arrest the small henchdog himself? *Was* there a henchdog?

Inside the tent, I heard Jack Johnson tell Shuffle to go away.

"Jack? What are you doing here?"

I Jack-jumped around. Foxy was peering out from under the tent wall.

"I'm looking for you!" I said.

"Did you arrest that bulldog?"

"He's innocent," I said. "What have *you* been doing?"

"I've been admiring a master sausage thief at work," said Foxy. "That dog is so smart!"

"Why haven't you barked for backup?" I asked.

"That dog is an artist," said Foxy. "He's working with a pug now. A while ago, it was a dachshund. Why not in-terrier-gate the pug, Jack?"

"I'd rather see this smart dog."

"OK," said Foxy. "Watch the sausages, Jack. Bark for backup if you see the pupetrator."

I steaked-out the front of the tent and watched the sausage boxes.

Jack and Jill Johnson kept telling me to go away. I ig-gnawed them. Foxy must be mistaken. A terrier could Jack-jump to the sausage boxes, but Jack and Jill Johnson would notice.

"Jack!" Lord Red ran into the middle of my steak-out. "Foxy says a clever small dog is planning a sausage heist!"

"Hush!" I scolded. "Don't tell the world!"

Red's ears drooped. "I have to tell *everyone*! Foxy said so!"

"Oh, did he?" I snapped. "Just who is in charge of this Sausage Situation?"

"Foxy said *he* was," said Red.

"This is getting out of paw," I growled.

Jack's Glossary

Henchdog. *A dog that is a partner in crime.*

Pawfectly. *Perfectly, only used for dogs.*

Pan-dog-monium

Before I could act, Shuffle wheezed into my steak-out.

Jack's Facts

If a Jack Russell terrier wheezes, it is sick.
If a pug wheezes, it is just being a pug.
That is a fact.

"Jack, a clever small dog is about to steal some sausages!" wheezed Shuffle. "I want to find that smart dog.

I'll ask him for some sausages."

"Yes!' chimed in Red. "I want to meet him, too. Can you detect him, Jack?"

"That's just what I'm doing!" I explained.

Red rushed away. "Clever dog!" I heard him calling. "Clever little dog! Where are you? Can I have a sausage?"

"**Bath water**!" I said. "He's going to ruin everything!"

"If Red is getting a sausage, I want a sausage, too," said Shuffle. "See you later, Jack."

I returned to Foxy's steak-out. "Are you out of your mind?" I said. "Why did you tell Red and Shuffle about this clever small dog?"

"Why not? The more dogs on the job, the better!" said Foxy.

"All this fuss will alert the pupetrator!" I reminded him. "Too many dogs will get in one another's way when the crime goes down."

"Jack!" Ralf Boxer bounced under my belly and nipped my toe. "Shuffle says a smart dog will give everyone sausages. He doesn't know who it is. I want to know."

"We all want to know," I growled. There was something pawfully wrong here.

Think, Jack! I told myself. *I am smart. So is Jill Russell. So is Polly Smote.*

I ticked off the clever, small dogs I knew in Doggeroo. None of them was a thief.

"It is a very clever Chihuahua,"

yapped Ralf Boxer. "We small dogs never get the recognition we deserve!"

"When you find out, tell Jack," said Foxy. "Spread the word! This situation could break any second!"

After Ralf Boxer had gone, the squekes appeared, yipping for information.

"Stop it, Foxy," I growled. "Everything is getting out of paw!"

Foxy didn't answer. He pointed toward the dog-toy tent. "Sausages! Sausages! Sausages!" he yapped.

"Where? Where? Where?" yipped the squekes.

"Didn't you see?" yapped Foxy, darting across the grass. "There he goes! Stop that sausage dog!"

In seconds, all the dogs were

barking as loudly as Foxy.

"There! Where?"

"The toy tent—see?"

"Where?"

"Catch that dog!"

"What dog?"

"A CLEVER DOG HAS TAKEN
ALL THE SAUSAGES!"

The hunt was on. Dogs were
everywhere, barking and passing on
the news. People tripped over them
and yelled. A pile of terriers leaped
into a bin of rubber bones, and fifteen
bouncy balls hopped all over the
ground.

Red pounced on one, and the
three squekes yipped over a plastic
squeaker chop.

Foxy rushed in circles, as if he was

trying to catch his tail. He seemed to have gone crazy.

Jack and Jill Johnson raced out of the tent, waving their tongs.

"Watch out!" cried Gloria Smote, and tripped over Shuffle, who was biting into a dropped hot dog.

Jack Johnson tried to grab Foxy as he scooted by, but Foxy doubled back and vanished into the pile of dogs.

It was **pan-dog-monium**!

Red dropped the ball and galloped up to me. "Where's the smart sausage dog, Jack? Where?"

"Over here!" yapped Ralf Boxer.

I ran after Ralf Boxer. Jack and Jill Johnson ran after us, followed by Caterina Smith, Dora Barkins, Sarge, and just about everyone else. The pan-dog-monium was getting worse.

There was going to be a terrier-able disaster if someone didn't take matters in paw. Sarge was doing his best, but Sarge is not a dog. This called for strong measures by a strong pack leader. And I knew just the dog for the job!

Jack's Glossary

Bath water. *One of the worst swearwords I know.*

Pan-dog-monium. *A lot of noise that involves dogs.*

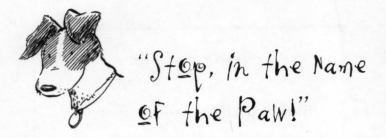

"Stop, in the Name of the Paw!"

Jack's Facts

Jack Russell terriers are not big dogs.
Occasionally this is a disadvantage.
A clever Jack can solve this problem
with ease.
This is a fact.

    I Jack-jumped onto the roof of the
tallest deluxe doghouse and surveyed
the situation. Someone, or something,
was at the bottom of this pan-dog-
monium. I considered the dogs I

knew. None of them had ever been mixed up with this kind of skulldoggery.

Maybe it was a dog I didn't know. I sniffed the air.

I couldn't detect any strange dog smells. Nor could I see any dogs I didn't know.

I was terrier-ably **paw-plexed** until I realized I couldn't see one dog I *did* know.

Where was Foxy?

Foxy should have been here. Surely he wanted to be in on the arrest of the clever sausage thief?

"Where's Foxy?" I yapped to Lord Red as he sailed by. Red didn't hear. He was still telling everyone about sausages and smart dogs.

I balanced on my hind legs on the

deluxe doghouse. I couldn't see Foxy. I
even Jack-jumped a few times. No
Foxy.

I pricked my ears, but I couldn't
hear Foxy.

Quickly, I made a nose map.

Jack's Map

1. Lots of dogs.

2. Lots of people.

3. Foxy.

4. Sausages.

5. Onions.

I turned around slowly, sniff-sniffing until I got a good direction. Aha! The scent of Foxy was coming from the tent.

The sausage thief must have returned to the tent under cover of the pan-dog-monium. Foxy must have seen the pupetrator and tracked it back to the tent. I had to get there quickly to make the arrest!

I Jack-jumped off the deluxe doghouse and hit something hairy on the way down. Lord Red yelped.

"I'm under attack! I'm being dognapped! Help, Jack!"

I bounced to my feet. No time to stop and talk to Red now. The case was about to break wide open.

I dived under Red's belly and raced back toward the tent.

Ralf Boxer got in my way, but I jumped over him and nearly landed on Shuffle.

"I've been mugged!" snuffled Shuffle. He yelped. Ralf Boxer had bitten his toe.

I dashed past my old steak-out and through the entrance of the tent, then skidded to a halt.

I knew just what I would see . . . and there it was. A box of sausages had been knocked off the table. It had burst open on the ground.

Sausages were hanging out in long, delicious strings.

Foxy was squatting on a pile of buttered bread, guzzling and feasting.

"Stop, in the name of the paw!" I commanded.

My pal went right on guzzling.

"Foxy, STOP!" I barked. "You're letting the pupetrator get away!"

I could see what had happened. Foxy had come to make an arrest, but the sight of the sausages had been too much for him. He had stopped for a snack while the pupetrator made his getaway.

"Foxy!" I snapped. "Pull yourself together! Which way did he go?"

Foxy burped and ate another sausage.

"What are you *doing?*" I asked.

"Eating my sausages," said Foxy through a mouthful. "Go away, Jack."

Jack's Glossary

Paw-plexed. *Perplexed and puzzled.*

Foxy Logic

That was almost the end of the Sausage Situation.

Since Foxy wouldn't listen to reason, I had a quick **Jack-snack** and then barked for backup. Jack and Jill Johnson and Sarge came back, but Foxy had already eaten a dozen sausages.

Auntie Tidge had to take him home.

I enjoyed the rest of Dog and Sausage Day. Lord Red was right. When there is no **skulldoggerer** around, games and sausages are fun!

Sarge and I got to judge the pet parade. The bulldog in the bonnet won. His prize was a day at a dog spa.

"Good!" he said. "What's a dog spa?"

"Soap," I said. "Shampooch. Clippers."

The bulldog snarled. "I'll get you for this, toothpick!"

All the runners-up got a chew toy and a sausage, and afterward, Sarge bought me a new squeaker-bone.

Foxy was pretty sick that night, so I left the official in-terrier-gation until the next day.

"What was all that **dogwash** about a clever small dog heisting sausages?" I demanded.

"It wasn't dogwash. It was true," said Foxy. His belly rumbled, and he groaned.

74

"No, Foxy. *You* took the sausages. There never was a clever small dog in the case. You made that up."

Foxy growled at me. "I am a clever dog. I am a small dog. And I wasn't stealing. I was *preventing* a crime."

He hiccuped.

"Foxy . . ."

"Look," said Foxy. "Those sausages were on the ground in my terrier-tory. That makes them rightfully mine. The only way I could keep them safe was by eating them."

He burped.

"You said the bulldog was working with you. Then you said you were working with a pug and a dachshund."

"Of paws!" said Foxy. "They all distracted the criminals while I laid my clever plot."

"But there were no criminals!"
I snapped. "Except for you!"

"Jack and Jill Johnson had my
sausages. That makes them criminals."

I stared at my pal. Foxy? Clever?
Maybe he was, but I couldn't follow
his logic.

Just then, Auntie Tidge came out
of the house, carrying a bowl. "Foxy
Woxy, I have some leftover sausages
here. Would you like some for dinner?"

Foxy looked sick. "Go away," he